first Day

To Susan—a very special person,
who can still enjoy books like a child

Margaret K. McElderry Books
An imprint of Simon & Schuster Children's Publishing Division
1230 Avenue of the Americas
New York, NY 10020
Copyright © 2002 by Joan Rankin
First published in 2002 in the United Kingdom by the Bodley Head Children's Books
as *Oh, Mum, I Don't Want to Go to School!*
First U.S. Edition 2002
Published by arrangement with the Bodley Head, the Random House Group Ltd.,
and the Inkman, Cape Town, South Africa
Printed in Singapore
2 4 6 8 10 9 7 5 3 1

Library of Congress Cataloging-in-Publication Data
Rankin, Joan.
First day / Joan Rankin.
p. cm.
Summary: Little Haybillybun is not the only one who is worried about the first day of preschool.
ISBN 0-689-84563-4
[1. First day of school—Fiction. 2. Nursery schools—Fiction. 3. Schools—Fiction.
4. Dogs—Fiction. 5. Animals—Fiction.] I. Title.
PZ7.R16815 Fi 2002
[E]—dc21
2001030852

first Day

Joan Rankin

Margaret K. McElderry Books

New York   London   Toronto   Sydney   Singapore

It was Haybillybun's first day of school.

"Wakey, wakey!" called his mother.

"Oh, Mom!" groaned Haybillybun. "Do I *have* to go to special Yappy Puppy Play School?"

"Yes, dear, you'll like it!" said Mom.

"No, I won't," moaned Haybillybun.

"I've got **slip-slidey-fluffy feet** and I won't be able to run at school. I'll fall off the jungle gym."

"You have lovely feet," replied his mother. "You'll be fine."

"*No, I won't,*" moaned Haybillybun.

"I've got **horrible fuzzy ears!**" wailed Haybillybun. "I won't be able to hear a word the teacher says."

"You can hear everything," said his mother.

"WHAAT?" asked Haybillybun.

"I said, 'Would you like a Chockie Bone in your lunch box?'" asked Mom, smiling.

"Oh yes, please, Mom!" said Haybillybun.

"Nobody listens to me. Nobody understands me,"
moaned Haybillybun.

"Hurry up!" called his mother. "It's getting late."

"I've got **scary** eyes! Nobody will play with me!"

"Well, why don't you wear your rock-'n'-roll sunglasses? Then everyone will play with you," suggested his dad.

"Oh, Mom!" said Haybillybun. "You're much bigger than I am. Can't you go to school for me?"

"Then you'll miss all the fun," said Mom.

"You can tell me all about it when you get home," said Haybillybun.

"All right," said Mom. "If you stay home and wash the dishes and make the beds and clean out the birdcage, then do the shopping and cook dinner, I'll go to school."

"Oh, Mom!"

Halfway to school, Haybillybun said,

"Mom, I've got such a LONG name.

When they arrived at school, Mom said, "This is Bun."

"Hello, Bun!" said the teacher. "These are your classmates."

Willywobbleknees

Pipsqueaker

Ginghamgumball

Ellajellybrolly

Jeremiahthunderbolt

Susieshyshoes

Haybillybun stayed at school,

and

his

mother

went

home . . .

to the dirty dishes,

and the oofy, poofy
birdcage.

Then she went upstairs to the rumpled beds.

And when she finally got to Haybillybun's bed,

she sighed a **big** sigh.

So she went to make a cup of tea and
sat down to think. "My poor Haybillybun!
He is much too small
to be away from home."

Quick as a flash, Haybillybun's mother put on her hat
and rushed off to the Yappy Puppy Play School.

Haybillybun's mom was going to **rescue** her darling boy.

When she got to the school, she peeped through the fence,

and this
is what
she saw . . .

She sneaked into the school yard

and crept around the school . . .

until she found a box to stand on.
She peeked into the window

and this is what she saw...

My Haybillybun is doing just fine, thought his mother.

Haybillybun's mother waited with the other parents
for the children to get out of school.

DING-DONG
The school bell rang,
and out ran the children.

"Look, Mom! Look what I painted!"

When they got home, Haybillybun
and his mother looked at his painting.
"Tell me about it," said Mom.
"This is me and Susieshyshoes on the slide.
This is me playing tag with
Ginghamgumball and
Willywobbleknees."

"And here is Ellajellybrolly, Jeremiahthunderbolt, and Pipsqueaker on the jungle gym," explained Haybillybun.

"And who is that at the top?" asked Dad.
"That's me!" said Haybillybun, proudly.

"What a lot of fun!" said Mom. "Can I go to school with you tomorrow?"

"Oh, Mom!" laughed Haybillybun, wriggling his lovely furry feet.